The Double Dabble Surprise

Beverly Lewis

Beverly Lewis Books for Young Readers

PICTURE BOOKS

In Jesse's Shoes
Just Like Mama • *What Is God Like?*
What Is Heaven Like?

THE CUL-DE-SAC KIDS

The Double Dabble Surprise
The Chicken Pox Panic
The Crazy Christmas Angel Mystery
No Grown-ups Allowed
Frog Power
The Mystery of Case D. Luc
The Stinky Sneakers Mystery
Pickle Pizza
Mailbox Mania
The Mudhole Mystery
Fiddlesticks
The Crabby Cat Caper
Tarantula Toes
Green Gravy
Backyard Bandit Mystery
Tree House Trouble
The Creepy Sleep-Over
The Great TV Turn-Off
Piggy Party
The Granny Game
Mystery Mutt
Big Bad Beans
The Upside-Down Day
The Midnight Mystery

Katie and Jake and the Haircut Mistake

www.BeverlyLewis.com

THE CUL-DE-SAC KIDS

The Double Dabble Surprise

Beverly Lewis

BETHANY HOUSE PUBLISHERS
MINNEAPOLIS, MINNESOTA 55438

© 1993 by Beverly Lewis

Originally published by Star Song Publishing Group
under the same title

Published by Bethany House Publishers
11400 Hampshire Avenue South
Bloomington, Minnesota 55438

Bethany House Publishers is a division of
Baker Publishing Group, Grand Rapids, Michigan

Printed in the United States of America by
Bethany Press International, Bloomington, MN
September 2014, 30th printing

ISBN 978-1-55661-625-9

Library of Congress Cataloging-in-Publication Data
Lewis, Beverly.
The double dabble surprise / Beverly Lewis.
    p.   cm. — (The cul-de-sac kids ; 1)
Summary: When their new Korean sisters do not arrive at the
airport, Abby and Carly have a mystery to solve, with God's help.
ISBN 1-55661-625-2
[1. Korean American—Fiction. 2. Brothers and sisters—Fiction. 3. Christian life—Fiction.] I. Title. II. Series: Lewis, Beverly. Cul-de-sac kids ; 1.
PZ7.L58464Do 1994
[Fic]—dc20   94-49116

Interior illustrations by Barbara Birch

14 15 16 17 18 17 18   36 35 34 33 32 31 30

To the memory
of my little friend

SKIPP CHOON GEUN

who now lives in a heavenly
cul-de-sac paved with gold.

THE CUL-DE-SAC KIDS

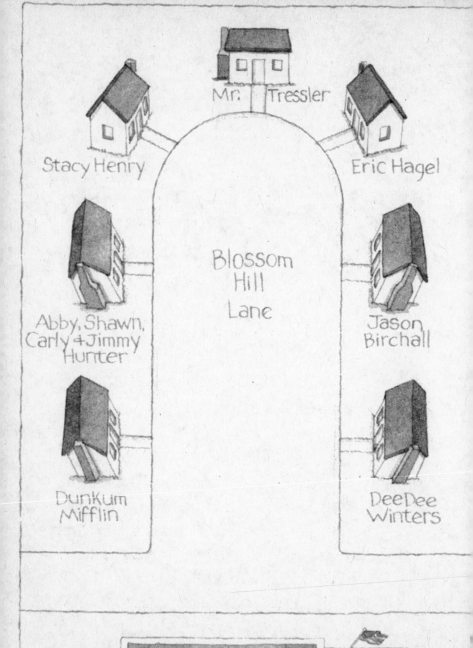

ONE

Abby Hunter drew an X with her red marker.

The X looked perfect on her teddy bear calendar.

"Next Saturday is the BIG day," she said. "In one week we'll meet our new sisters from Korea."

She made dancing stars around the red X.

"I can't wait," said Carly, her little sister, looking up from her first grade spelling list.

Abby snapped the cap on her marker. "Just think, there will be four girls in our family."

"I think Daddy wanted some boys," Carly said.

"Mommy doesn't know how to raise boys," Abby said. "There aren't any boys in her family for three generations."

Carly twisted one of her blonde curls. "What's a generator?"

Abby sighed. "Not generator—generation."

"Well, what is it?" Carly asked.

"It's all the kids born in a family. When they get old—about thirty—those kids get married and have kids. Then those kids . . ."

"Okay, I get it," Carly said.

Abby straightened her calendar. "*That's* why we only have girl cousins."

Carly wrote a spelling word. "I'm glad generator isn't on this list!"

"Generation," Abby insisted.

"Whatever," said Carly. She made a tic-tac-toe on her paper. "Wanta play?"

"Can't," Abby said. "Dunkum is coming over to shoot baskets."

Dunkum was the best player in Abby's third grade class. His real name was Edward Mifflin, but no one called him that.

2

"Dunkum thinks he can't be beat, but I'm trying," Abby said.

"Is Dunkum your best friend?" Carly asked, looking down at Abby's sneakers. One was red and one was blue.

"Maybe," Abby whispered.

The doorbell rang, followed by pounding on the front door.

Abby grabbed her jacket. "That's definitely Dunkum."

Carly sighed. "When our Korean sisters come, maybe they'll play with me."

★　★　★

After lunch the girls helped their mother put up a pink wall hanging. It read: WEL-COME SISTERS.

"Soon, I'll have three sisters," Abby said.

Carly jumped up and down. "Just in time for Thanksgiving."

"Before," corrected Abby. "Thanksgiving's in twelve days."

3

"Carly, please hold your end still," said Mother.

"She's too excited," said Abby.

They stepped back to admire the wall hanging. It looked perfect in their soon-to-be new sisters' bedroom.

Now the room was ready. Matching pink spreads covered the beds. Fancy curtains and bows covered the windows.

"I like this room better than mine," Carly said.

Abby swung her sister around. "I'll trade *your* room for mine."

"Nope," Carly said.

Abby had Carly's room when she was little. There was a secret place in the closet. A *secret*, secret place. She missed hiding there with a flashlight and a good book.

Now Carly had the room. And the secret place.

Sometimes Abby and Carly hid there together. Abby would read softly to Carly.

Mother often forgot to look for them, in the secret place behind the closet.

"Meet me in five seconds," Abby whispered.

"Where?" Carly said.

"In the secret place," Abby said. "We have secret plans to make."

Carly's eyes shone. "Okay!" she said, and she dashed out of the room.

Abby hoped things wouldn't change too much when her Korean sisters arrived next Saturday.

But . . . she would wait before sharing the secret place with them. Just a little while.

TWO

Abby pulled a pillow into the secret place.

"Shh! Don't make a sound." She slid the skinny door shut.

Abby switched on two flashlights. One for Carly. One for herself.

"Call the meeting to order," Carly whispered.

"Okay. The meeting will come to order. Now, is there any news?"

"Nope," Carly said. "Get to the important stuff. What's the secret plan?"

"Let's buy welcome-home presents for our new sisters."

"Like what?" Carly said.

"Let's buy matching bears—bride bears!" Abby said.

"With lots of white lace." Carly wiggled all over.

Abby twirled her flashlight. "Mommy and Daddy will be surprised, too."

Carly grinned. "If we keep it a secret."

"When Daddy buys gas for the car, we'll ride along," Abby said. She planned every-thing. She always did.

Abby had another idea. "Let's make cards for our sisters, too."

"Out of pink paper," Carly said.

"And lace from Mommy's sewing box," Abby said.

Carly clapped her hands. "To match the bears' gowns."

The girls did their hand-over-hand secret code. Then they prayed.

"Dear Lord," Abby began. "We're getting new sisters."

"They might not know about you," Carly added.

Abby finished the prayer. "Please help us show Your love to them. In Jesus' name, Amen."

They turned off the flashlights and crawled out of the closet.

Abby curled up on Carly's bed and cuddled two teddy bears.

Carly looked worried. "What about our secret place? Can we keep it a secret from our new sisters?"

"Definitely," Abby said. "But not for *too* long."

Carly looked like she was going to cry.

"What's wrong?" Abby said. She moved close to her sister.

"I'm afraid you won't be my best friend anymore," Carly whimpered.

She hugged her bear. "Maybe you'll like our new sisters better."

"Don't be silly," Abby said, patting Carly's hair. She wished her own hair would grow. Long and curly like Carly's.

"Let's make a braid," Abby said.

"Goody!" Carly said. She hopped off the bed to get some hair ribbons.

"Make four braids," Carly begged.

"Four will look silly," Abby said.

Carly pouted. "Come on, Abby. Just for fun?"

Abby tossed the hair ribbons onto the bed. She stomped out of Carly's room. She could hear Carly yelling for Mother.

Let her tattle. Abby didn't care.

It would be great having a sister who wasn't such a baby.

THREE

Abby put the bride bears in a yellow basket.

"I'll carry it," Carly said.

Abby slid the welcome-home cards into the basket.

Carly twisted her hair. "Do you think they've seen bride bears before?"

"Maybe. Maybe not. There will be lots of stuff in America they've never seen."

"When will we give the presents?" Carly asked.

"You'll see," Abby said. She wished Carly would stop asking so many questions.

★　★　★

The airport buzzed with people. Some carried suitcases. Others pushed carts and pulled luggage.

Mrs. Roop, the caseworker, spotted the airline schedule. "Flight 225 is late." She pointing at the screen above their heads.

Abby and Carly groaned.

"Let's have some dessert while we wait," Mother suggested.

They strolled toward the snack shop.

"Show us the pictures again," Abby said after dessert.

Her father pulled out pictures of two Korean girls.

Carly stood on tiptoes to see the pictures. "Will they get homesick?"

"Our home will soon become their home," her father said. "We want to make things easy for them. You and Abby can help us." He hugged Carly.

"We'll help them learn our ways, Daddy," Abby said.

Carly nodded. "And God's ways. We promise."

Abby couldn't wait to give the bride bears to her new sisters.

She remembered getting her first bear dressed as a bride two years ago, at Christmas. Her father had read the Christmas story from the Bible on Christmas Eve. Everyone opened one present. They saved the rest for Christmas morning.

Abby's was a bride bear. It had a tiny red bow on its veil.

That same Christmas, Abby's parents had told them the plan to adopt Korean girls. It was a long wait. Too long for Abby. She had always wished for another sister closer to her own age. Soon she would have that sister. Carly would too.

Abby thought the hour would never end. She leaned against her mother, who seemed tired. Maybe the waiting bothered her, too.

At last, flight 225 arrived. The Hunter family raced to gate B-7. Abby arrived first.

The waiting area was full of families and caseworkers. All of them waited to welcome Korean kids to America.

Abby watched the kids and their escorts stand in line, showing their passports.

She held her breath. There were hundreds of people. How would they find their sisters? Or Miss Lin, the escort who brought them from Korea?

This could definitely be a problem, Abby thought.

Definitely.

FOUR

Abby spun around. Her parents and Mrs. Roop stood behind her. "Quick! Get the pictures out." She tugged on her father's coat sleeve.

"We know what our sisters look like," Carly insisted.

But Abby wanted to be double sure.

"We'll stay here and wait for the escort," her father said. He unfolded a paper square and gave it to Abby. On the paper were the words: HUNTER FAMILY.

"Great idea, Daddy," Abby said, holding it high. "I'm going to explode if we don't see them soon."

"Be patient, dear," Mrs. Roop said. "It won't be much longer."

"I can't wait," Abby said. "Come on, Carly, let's go look for them." She handed the sign to her father, but kept the pictures. Grabbing Carly's hand, Abby led the way through the crowd.

In the far corner sat two girls.

Abby studied the girls, then the pictures. "What do you think?" she asked Carly.

"Maybe they grew a lot."

Abby inched closer. She saw the name tag on the escort. It was not Miss Lin. Abby felt brave. "Excuse me, do you know who Miss Lin is?"

The lady smiled. "Are you getting a new sister?"

"Two," Abby said. She felt like a jitterbox inside.

The lady pointed. "Miss Lin is over there."

"Thank you," Abby said, looking. She stood stone still. "Something's crazy wrong," she whispered.

16

Carly came closer. "What is?"

"Can't you see? Miss Lin is with two *boys!*"

The girls stared.

"Let's find our *sisters*," Abby said. She walked up to Miss Lin.

Carly followed.

Miss Lin knew nothing about sisters. She introduced the boys. "I'd like you to meet Li Sung Jin and his little brother, Li Choon Koo," she said.

Carly reached out to shake hands.

Abby turned away. She hurried to find her parents and Mrs. Roop. "Daddy! Mommy! Come quick! Something's crazy wrong!"

They pushed through the crowd and found Miss Lin again. She introduced the boys who bowed to Abby's parents.

Mrs. Roop studied some papers. So did Miss Lin.

Abby watched her mother's face turn pale. She was puzzled at the twinkle in her father's eyes.

The Korean boys sat down and waited.

17

They looked stiff and scared as Abby's father led Mrs. Roop around the corner.

Abby stared at the boys' black hair. It was dark blue. The younger boy was skinny. She couldn't see a single muscle on him. Not one.

The older boy had sad eyes. He played with a shiny round tag. He seemed to be in charge of his little brother, Choon Koo.

Abby walked around behind the seat for a better look. She was dying to see Sung Jin's silver tag.

What is it? she wondered.

Both boys sat as straight as boards.

At last the grown-ups returned.

"Let's take a walk," Mother suggested.

The Hunter family huddled in the hallway.

"There's been a mistake," Mr. Hunter explained.

"But I . . . uh . . . we don't want brothers," Abby said.

"Your sisters will arrive in three days." He put his arms around Abby and Carly.

"What about the boys?" Carly asked.

18

Mother answered, "They will stay with us until Mrs. Roop clears up the mistake."

"We have to *keep* them?" Abby cried.

"It's only three days," said her father.

"Oh, no!" Abby shouted. "Where will they sleep?"

"In the new room," Mother said softly.

"Not our *sisters'* room," Abby said. She pushed the presents down in the basket. She looked at Carly. "Keep the bears hidden."

"Good idea," said Carly. "But what kind of gifts can we give them?"

Father smiled. "What about kindness? That's one gift these boys could use right now."

Abby stared at the floor. "They won't want bride bears, that's for sure," she said.

Her throat felt lumpy. *This can't be happening,* she thought.

FIVE

Abby lagged behind as Sung Jin and Choon Koo walked between her parents, down the long hallway.

Abby's father talked to them. They seemed to understand English. Choon Koo kept nodding—not talking.

Carly giggled. She pointed to a crop of hair sticking straight out on Choon Koo's head.

Abby poked her. "Shh!"

Abby stared at Sung Jin's wrinkled shorts and T-shirt. *He must have slept in them*, she thought. *Boys! How will I ever get through the next three days?*

They waited for Father to bring the car around.

Abby set the yellow basket down.

Choon Koo stared at the shiny paper peeking out. He bent down to look inside. "Pret-ty pa-per," he said slowly.

Before Abby could stop him, he pulled a present out. His brother spoke to him in Korean.

Choon Koo held the present up. He turned it over and over.

Abby wished her mother would do something.

In a flash the wrapping paper was off! A bride bear smiled up at Choon Koo.

Abby thought she would choke.

Sung Jin grabbed the bear away from his brother. He turned it around and around, giggling.

Abby looked at Mother. "Stop them!" she cried.

Mother raised a finger to her lips.

★　★　★

On the ride home, Choon Koo balanced a bear bride on his feet. So did Sung Jin. Then they bounced the bears on their sandals, pointing and giggling.

The giggling bugged Abby. And the bears would be dirty when her sisters finally came. *Phooey!*

Carly turned around in the front seat. Her eyes got big.

Abby looked away. She couldn't wait to get home. "How many more minutes?" she asked her father.

"Be polite, honey," he said.

Polite. Usually that was easy. But not today! Today she would call her friend, Stacy Henry. Maybe Stacy would let her move in for three days.

Besides, Stacy owed her a favor. A double-dabble favor.

Last month, when she covered for Stacy at

23

recess, a stray puppy had wandered onto the playground. He looked sick and sad. He needed help. Stacy had whispered her plan to Abby.

Abby talked to the playground teacher while Stacy hid the sick cock-a-poo under her jacket. She sneaked to the edge of the playground. Then she raced home with him, three houses away.

Later, Abby had helped Stacy talk her mother into keeping the cuddly white puppy.

It was a double dabble favor.

"We're home," shouted Carly.

The boys leaned forward to look.

Abby couldn't wait to get to the phone. *Stacy will help me*, thought Abby. *The Cul-de-sac kids always stick together!*

She ran into the house—away from the boys.

SIX

Inside, Abby grabbed the phone. She told Stacy about the boys and the crazy mix-up.

"What will you do?" Stacy said.

"I'll call Dunkum," Abby said. "He can teach them to shoot baskets. That could take three days." She laughed.

Carly ran into the kitchen. "The boys undressed the bride bears," Carly whispered in Abby's other ear.

"Yikes! Gotta go." Abby hung up the phone and hurried upstairs.

The boys' door was open. Abby stopped in the hallway. She couldn't believe what she saw.

Sung Jin was dancing with a wedding dress on his head. "Dance," he said. "Dance!"

He twirled around. Faster and faster. The white lace dress slid off his head.

Abby caught it. "This goes on the bears for our sisters."

Sung Jin looked around. "Sisters?" He pointed to Carly. "She is sister."

"Our *new* sisters are coming in three days." Under her breath Abby said, "They better come."

Choon Koo came running out of the closet! He held up a girl's slip and waved the hanger around as he giggled. Then he jumped onto one of the beds. He pulled at the bows on the curtain.

"Be careful," Abby said. "The curtains will fall down."

"Down, down. Take them down," he chanted. "I don't like."

Sung Jin walked out of the room. Choon Koo climbed off the bed and followed his brother.

27

Abby held her breath. She felt like a jitterbox—all shaky inside.

Carly chased after the boys.

Abby looked down at the bedroom rug.
Something shiny was lying there. She leaned
down. It was Sung Jin's round tag!

Strange marks were on each side. *This
must be Korean writing,* thought Abby. She
slipped the silver tag into her pocket.

Abby went to the kitchen. Mother was
cooking with the new rice cooker.

Abby sniffed the air. "What's for supper?"

"Rice," Mother said. "And kimchi.

Abby pinched her nose. "Smells terrible."

"The boys will like it," Mother said.

Abby groaned. "Will our sisters like it,
too?"

Mother nodded.

"What's in this kimchi stuff?" Abby said.

"You'll eat better if you don't know,"
Mother said, smiling.

"Sounds scary. What else are we having?"

"Hot dogs, baked beans and chips," Mother said.

"That's what *I'm* having." Abby ran to find Carly. She had to warn her not to eat the Korean food. It smelled rotten.

Carly was outside on the driveway with the boys. The Cul-de-sac Kids were there, too.

Dunkum dribbled his basketball. He showed off his fancy moves.

Jason Birchall chased behind Dunkum trying to grab the ball. He was hyper, as always.

Stacy Henry showed off her puppy. Carly played with his floppy ears.

Dee Dee Winters sneaked a suck on her thumb.

Eric Hagel showed up on his hot ten-speed. "What's up?"

"Let's have a meeting." Abby said.

Dunkum shot another basket. "Right now?"

Carly squealed, "Wow! Nine in a row!"

"Let's get acquainted with the new boys on the block," said Stacy.

Sung Jin and Choon Koo turned toward each other. Choon Koo reached for his big brother.

Abby felt sad. She wondered how it felt being stuck with a family who didn't want boys.

Then she dug into her jeans pocket and handed the silver tag to Sung Jin. His sad eyes lit up.

"This must've fallen when you danced," Abby said.

Sung Jin held it tightly. "Thank you," he said.

Then Abby had an idea. A double dabble—definitely good idea.

SEVEN

Abby called the kids over to the porch. "Let's help Sun Jin and Choon Koo get to know us. Everyone tell your name and how old you are," she said.

"And pig-out foods," yelled Jason Birchall.

The kids laughed as they sat on the porch.

"Leave it to Abby," Eric said. He put the kickstand down on his bike.

"I'll go first," Dunkum offered.

The kids stretched their necks when Dunkum stood.

Choon Koo said, "Very tall boy."

Dunkum told his name. "I'm a third grade

health freak. I eat salads with alfalfa sprouts and tomatoes."

"Oo-ee!" Carly squealed, holding her nose.

Dunkum stretched his arms. "They make me grow tall. Tall enough to dunk the ball. Almost."

The kids cheered.

"Who's next?" Abby asked.

"I am." Carly said her name with Anne in the middle. "I'm in first grade, and I'm starting to dream about rice." She grinned at Choon Koo. He laughed his high giggle.

Sung Jin sat straight and still. "I am Li Sung Jin, age nine. I like American rice."

Choon Koo jumped up. "I like Jimmy name." He patted his chest. "I now am Jimmy. Jimmy eat. Jimmy eat and eat rice."

Abby couldn't believe it. Choon Koo *looked* like a Jimmy. "Jimmy," she said, pointing to him. "Pick someone."

He pointed to Stacy Henry. She held up her puppy. "This is Sunday Funnies. He finds the funnies every Sunday before anyone else."

Dee Dee giggled.

Stacy continued. "I'm in third. I like pizza the best. We only have it on weekends."

Abby pointed to Dee Dee. "Your turn," she said.

"I'm Dee Dee Winters." She wiped off her wet thumb. "I'm in first grade, and chocolate ice cream is my favorite. I don't know why. It just is." Dee Dee sat down. She looked at Eric.

"Hi, I'm Eric Hagel. We moved here from Germany two years ago. I'm in Abby's class, third grade." He paused and smiled at her. "I eat sweet tarts. My grandpa has pockets full of them. He's the watchmaker up the street." Eric sat down beside Dunkum.

"Sweet tarts aren't real food," Abby teased.

"Are so," Eric said. He threw her one.

She caught it.

"Where's mine?" Jason asked.

"You're not supposed to have sugar," Eric said. "Remember?"

Jason crossed his eyes. "My name's Jason

Allen Birchall. But my friends call me Jason."

Dee Dee popped out her thumb. "Nice name." She giggled.

"Now it's *your* turn," Eric told Abby.

She stood up. "Abby Hunter. Third grade. My favoite food is spaghetti. It slides down when I slurp it."

"Hurrah for spaghetti!" cheered Jason.

"Don't forget the grated cheese," yelled Dee Dee.

Then Abby said, "Sung Jin and Choon Koo will be here for only three days."

Choon Koo stood up. "Not Choon Koo. I *Jimmy.*"

Sung Jin pulled his brother back down.

"I forgot about your new name," Abby said. "I'm sorry." She really was.

"The kids on Blossom Hill Lane stick together no matter how long they stay," said Eric. "Welcome to our cul-de-sac."

Suddenly Sung Jin's eyes sparkled. The sadness was gone.

Abby's mother called for supper. Sung and Jimmy hurried inside.

Jason tried to invite himself, but then he smelled the kimchee. He held his nose instead. "Are we having a meeting next week?"

"When our Korean sisters come," Abby said.

She hoped it was soon. Very soon.

EIGHT

It was Monday morning.

Sung Jin and Jimmy (Choon Koo) sat on the porch swing ready for a visit to Blossom Hill School. They wore new American clothes.

Abby tied her sneakers in a double knot. One red. One blue.

Carly ran out of the house.

Abby led the way down the cul-de-sac. The kids came dashing out. At the corner, they bunched together to cross the street.

When they reached the school yard, Abby shouted, "Count-down to recess."

"Recess, recess," the kids chanted. Then they scattered in different directions.

Jimmy followed Carly and Dee Dee to first grade.

Sung Jin went with Abby and Stacy to third. Jason darted ahead of Eric and Dunkum.

In Math, Sung Jin tried the problems. He had trouble. The teacher gave him an easier paper. Kids bumped into each other trying to help him.

At recess, Jason saved a swing for Sung Jin. Eric asked Sung Jin to play soccer. Dunkum got dibs on lunch.

Abby and Stacy hung from the bars.

"Still want to move in?" Stacy asked.

"Guess not. Our sisters will be coming soon."

"What will happen to Jimmy and Sung Jin?" Stacy asked.

"I don't know. They're leaving with Mrs. Roop soon."

37

Abby hoped the boys would like their new family.

★　★　★

On the way home, Abby skipped over the sidewalk cracks.

The cul-de-sac boys yelled for Sung Jin and Jimmy to play basketball.

Carly went to Dee Dee's house.

Abby walked home alone.

In the house, Mother was cooking rice again.

Abby hurried to the secret place. Tomorrow, the best day. Her sisters were coming!

She flipped on the flashlight and slid the skinny door shut. Finding her Sunday school paper, she read the story. It was about secret sins.

She looked up Psalm 19:12 in her Bible. Abby felt funny inside. *How many secret sins do I have?* she wondered. She talked to God about it.

Later, Abby heard her parents talking. She crawled out of the closet to listen.

Mother sounded upset. "Mrs. Roop called this morning. She wants us to keep the boys another week."

"How do you feel about it, dear?" Abby's father asked.

"I really don't know," Mother said. "It will be harder for them to leave . . . the longer they stay."

Father chuckled. "They are having a great time, aren't they?"

"A great time tearing the bedroom apart," Mother said.

"It's not much of a boys' bedroom, now is it, dear?"

Is Daddy sticking up for them? Abby wondered.

Mother's voice shook. "Where are the girls? *Our girls?*"

Abby held her breath.

"Mrs. Roop is handling that," her father

said. "Let's trust the Lord to take care of things."

Scre-e-ech! Outside, a car slammed on its brakes.

Abby ran to the window. She saw Sunday Funnies limp away from the car and hide under Eric's porch.

Sung Jin chased the hurt puppy. He crawled under the porch and coaxed the puppy out. Then he took off his jacket.

Eric and Dunkum came running. Gently, they lifted the puppy into Sung Jin's jacket.

Abby dashed downstairs. "Mommy, come quick!" she called. "It's Sung, er, Stacy. I mean, it's Sunday Funnies."

Mother hurried outside to Sung Jin. "Are you all right?"

Sung Jin looked bashful, but he nodded.

"Sung's fine," called Jason from across the street. "The puppy's hurt."

The boys made a three-cornered stretcher with Sung's jacket. Slowly, step by step, they carried him across the street.

Stacy stroked Sunday Funnies as the driver got out of the car. His face was white. He looked at the puppy and patted his head.

The boys carried the puppy to Abby's mother. Stacy followed close behind.

"I'll call the vet," Mrs. Hunter said. She hurried inside the house.

Stacy followed. Abby held her hand.

Soon the kitchen was filled with kids. Droopy-faced kids.

Sung Jin and Eric and Dunkum laid Sunday Funnies on the floor. They knelt around him. Abby thought Stacy was praying.

Abby's mother called the vet.

Carly came into the house. "What happened?"

"Sunday Funnies got hit by a car," Abby said.

"Oh no!" she cried, sitting on the floor near the puppy.

Mother hung up the phone. "The vet wants to check him for a broken leg."

"I'll call my mom at work," Stacy said.

41

"She'll drive me to the vet. Thank you, Mrs. Hunter." Then she turned to Sung Jin. "Thank *you*. I'm going to miss you when you leave tomorrow."

After the kids were gone, Abby whispered to Carly, "Meet me in the secret place."

Inside the secret place, Abby told Carly about the boys staying longer.

"Another week?" said Carly. "Will we ever get our sisters?"

"I guess so," Abby said. "I hope so—I think."

NINE

The next day, Abby jumped a pretend hop-scotch while she waited for Stacy.

At last, Stacy skipped down her front steps.

"Hi," Abby said. "How's Sunday Funnies?"

"Limping a lot."

Abby kicked a stone down the sidewalk. "Lucky he didn't get killed."

"Poor thing," Stacy said. "I sneaked some waffles to help cheer him up. What did you have for breakfast?"

"Rice."

"Cream of rice?"

Abby sighed. "No, rice rice."

"You're kidding."

Abby laughed. "It's not so bad."

Stacy grinned. "How are the boys doing?"

"Sung Jin and Jimmy are learning to pray for their food," Abby said. "And Sung Jin keeps reminding God that he's eating *American* rice now."

"Do the boys know about Jesus?" asked Stacy.

"We teach them something new every day from the Bible. They'll have a good idea by the time they leave."

"What if they don't get a Christian family?" Stacy asked.

Abby hadn't thought of that. "I will pray that they do!"

"Will Sung Jin always have two names?" Stacy asked.

Abby hopped on one foot. "Only till he gets an American name," she said.

★   ★   ★

After school it was snowing fast. Abby scuffed her shoes on the snowy sidewalk.

Mother looked up from her Korean cookbook as Abby came into the kitchen.

"Is Carly home yet?" Abby asked.

"They were just here," her mother said.

"They?"

"Carly and Choon Koo."

"You mean Jimmy."

Mother closed the cookbook. "Who?"

"Choon Koo is Jimmy now."

"He can't choose his name," Mother said.

"But he *wants* to be called Jimmy."

"His parents will choose his name," her mother insisted.

Abby didn't like it. Choon Koo was Jimmy. He even looked like a Jimmy!

Abby peeked in Carly's room. No one there. She looked in the boys' room. "Oh no!" she wailed.

Bows were off the curtains. Bedspreads were rolled up and stuffed under the beds. The corners were sticking out.

46

The bride bears stood side-by-side on the bookcase. They looked like boy bears now. Each had a red paper hat stuck to its head.

Scissors and left-over scraps lay on the floor.

Dresser drawers hung open. Mother's pink wall hanging lay folded inside the bottom drawer.

Those horrible boys!

She turned to go, calling for Carly.

No answer.

She dashed to the secret place and slid open the skinny door.

There sat Carly reading to Jimmy.

"What are you doing?" Abby shouted.

"Helping Jimmy read," Carly said, shining the flashlight in Abby's face.

Abby frowned at her little sister. *Carly knows better. Jimmy doesn't belong in here!*

Abby churned with anger. She ran through the rain to Dunkum's next door to help him with his spelling.

Phooey! Carly had shared the secret place with Jimmy. Things were crazy wrong.

Definitely!

47

TEN

Later, Abby ran back home. She dashed to her sister's room. "How could you!"

"What?" Carly asked.

"You showed Jimmy our secret place!" Abby hollered.

"So what?"

Abby stared at Carly. "You didn't tell him our secret code did you?"

Carly frowned. "What's *wrong* with you, Abby?"

"Nothing."

Carly lined up her stuffed animals in a row on her bed. "Abby, why don't you like Jimmy and Sung Jin?"

Abby held her breath. "They aren't sisters," Abby said slowly. "That's why."

★ ★ ★

Wednesday at breakfast, Mother said, "Come home right after school. All bedrooms must be cleaned."

"Mine *is* clean," Carly said.

"Spotless?" Mother asked.

Carly nodded.

"What's the hurry?" Abby asked.

"Mrs. Roop is coming after supper," Mother said.

"What for?" Carly asked.

"For a visit," Mother said. She wiped the table.

"To check our rooms?" Carly asked.

Abby wished Carly would stop asking questions. She felt like a jitterbox again. Mother knew more than she was telling. She was sure of it.

Abby followed her mother downstairs. "It's about keeping the boys, isn't it?"

Mother sat on the sofa. She patted the pillow beside her. "How do you feel about that?"

Abby's brain was in a whirl. She felt all mixed up. "I like Jimmy and Sung Jin—it's not that. I just had my hopes on getting girls."

"I know, honey. So did I." Mother hugged Abby close. "Let's pray about it, okay?"

Abby nodded.

Later, she walked to school by herself. It was a good time to talk to God alone.

★ ★ ★

After supper, Mrs. Roop sat in the living room with Abby's parents. They talked for a long time.

Mrs. Roop visited Abby's room first. She closed the door and sat on the bed. She smelled like roses. "I like your green and yellow wallpaper. It's lovely."

Abby felt like a jitterbox.

Mrs. Roop asked questions about Sung Jin and Choon Koo.

"Choon Koo is Jimmy now," Abby said. *Why doesn't anyone pay attention?*

Mrs. Roop asked more questions. They made Abby even more jittery. "How would you like Sung Jin and Choon Koo, uh, Jimmy to be your brothers?"

"What about our sisters?" Abby asked.

"We've located them," she said. "The girls are still in Korea. Your parents will have to file papers again." She paused. "But the *boys* are happy here."

It sounded like a question without a question mark.

Abby wished she was alone in the secret place.

She couldn't wait for Mrs. Roop to leave.

★ ★ ★

Bath time. Jimmy was yelling. Ever since the first night in America, Jimmy hated

51

baths. Father gave him one anyway. Jimmy squealed louder and louder.

Maybe he's scared, thought Abby. She searched for her old plastic duck. She found it in a shoe box in her closet. Knocking on the bathroom door, Abby showed the duck to her father. "Will this help?"

Quickly, the squealing stopped.

After his bath, Jimmy brought the drippy duck to Abby.

"Keep it. It's yours," she said.

Jimmy hugged the duck.

Abby wanted to hug him, but she didn't.

Later, Sung Jin asked Abby if they could visit Stacy's puppy.

"We'll go after school tomorrow," Abby promised.

Sung Jin was grinning. *Really* grinning.

Abby wondered what it would be like having Sung Jin for a brother. But at bedtime, she prayed for her *sisters* in Korea.

ELEVEN

"School's out for Thanksgiving!" shouted Abby on the way to Stacy's house. She rang the doorbell. Sung Jin waited beside her on the snowy porch.

Soon the door swung wide. Stacy was carrying Sunday Funnies. His little splint looked like a toy.

Sung Jin stroked the puppy. "Better?"

"He's *much* better," Stacy said. "Thanks."

"I had puppy long, long time," Sung Jin said.

"In Korea?" Stacy asked.

"Before orphanage." Sung Jin's eyes looked sad again. "My puppy look like this."

Abby felt sorry for Sung Jin. Everything he loved was in Korea.

He pulled out the shiny round tag. "I keep this."

Abby saw the Korean marks on it. "What does it mean?"

"Hang-bok. In English, my puppy's name mean Happy."

Stacy smiled. "Just like Sunday Funnies. Good times, happy times."

Sung Jin giggled. The giggling didn't bother Abby today. She was glad to see Sung Jin having a good time. They played with Sunday Funnies until time for supper.

Later, after dishes were done, Abby sneaked to her father's study. She tapped on the door.

Abby held her breath. "I've decided something, Daddy."

"What is it, Abby?" He leaned back in his chair.

"I want us to adopt Sung Jin and Jimmy." Abby's eyes filled with happy tears.

"Bless your heart," her father said. He stood up and kissed Abby's cheek.

"And . . . I have an idea," said Abby.

Her father grinned. "What is it?"

"A double dabble Thanksgiving surprise!"

"It is?" he said, playing along.

So, it was settled. Tomorrow, Sung Jin and Jimmy would have a big surprise!

Early Thanksgiving morning, Abby helped Mother shine silver—knives, forks, and spoons. She set out bowls for the boys' kimchi, and plates for the turkey.

Sung Jin helped Abby with the decorations—pilgrim boys and girls. A pair for each end of the table.

He pointed to the pilgrims. "Who?"

"They're pilgrims. They came to America long ago. They wanted freedom to worship God."

Sung Jin looked puzzled. "Worship?"

Abby understood. Sung Jin had never heard the story of the first Thanksgiving.

She drew a picture of pilgrims sailing the

ocean in a big boat. "God kept the pilgrims safe when they came to America," she said. She made the waves swish around her boat.

"After a long winter, the pilgrims had a feast. They shared food with their new friends." Abby drew a long table with stick figures sitting with folded hands. "Here's how they worshipped God on the first Thanksgiving. They said thank you in a prayer."

Sung Jin's eyes grew wide. "I learn new things in America."

"I'm learning new things, too," Abby said. *About me,* she thought.

Mother came over to the table and looked at the drawings.

Sung Jin touched the pilgrim girl. "Abby, best sister. She tell first Thanksgiving story."

Abby felt warm inside.

Carly and Jimmy came in just then.

"The Cul-de-sac Kids are outside. They want to see Jimmy and Sung," Carly said.

Abby and Sung put on their jackets and hurried outdoors.

Dunkum bounced his ball on the snow-packed porch. Jason slid around trying to steal the ball.

Stacy stomped the snow off her feet. Sunday Funnies limped on his splint. Stacy picked him up and cuddled him.

Eric pulled Dee Dee on his sled. "Happy turkey day," he called.

Sung turned to look at Abby. There was a question in his dark eyes. "Turkey day?"

"Some people call it that because we eat turkey," Abby explained. "But the most important thing is to give thanks to God."

Eric pulled the sled up the driveway. He handed a bag of sweet tarts to Abby. "These are from my grandpa, for after dinner."

"Where's mine?" Jason asked, licking his lips.

"No snitching," Dee Dee hollered.

Jason groaned and rolled his eyes.

Dee Dee's nose wrinkled up at him.

Mother peeked out just then. "Family meeting time."

"Goody," Carly shouted.

Abby hoped the meeting was about adopting the boys. She couldn't wait to give them her big surprise!

TWELVE

Abby sat next to her father in the living room.

"Something important has happened," he began. "We are going to adopt Sung Jin and Choon Koo."

Abby clapped her hands. "Yip-p-e-ee!" she shouted.

Jimmy and Carly jumped up and down.

"We stay here?" Sung Jin asked.

"You certainly do," Father said. "We are very proud to adopt such fine boys."

Abby glanced at her mother. She was smiling, too.

"Sung Jin needs an American name,"

Mother said holding the family Bible. "We like the name Shawn."

Abby did too. It sounded something like Sung.

Mother wrote his new name in the Bible.

Jimmy leaped off his chair. "I am Jimmy. Yes?"

Mother laughed.

Father set Jimmy on his knee. "You are Jimmy Hunter."

Abby couldn't imagine any other name for him. She couldn't even imagine having more sisters. Not now.

"Bows come down," Jimmy said.

Father looked puzzled. "What does he mean?"

Abby knew. "He means the bows on their bedroom curtains."

"Yes," said Jimmy. "All girl things come down."

Mother nodded. "All frills must go. You and Sung, er . . . Shawn can help us change your room to look like a boy's room."

Jimmy danced a jig.

Shawn tossed his silver dog tag in the air. "Yes!"

Abby went to get the camera. Her father took pictures of all the kids.

"There's a surprise for you," Abby whispered to Shawn.

"Surprise?" Shawn's dark eyes sparkled.

"After dinner."

At the table, Father said to join hands. Everyone bowed heads for a Thanksgiving prayer.

When Amen was said, Shawn spoke up. "I say thank you to God for new family. Big thank you."

Abby smiled at him across the table.

After dinner, Abby met her father in his study. "Are we ready for the you-know-what?"

He hugged her. "It's just the right time."

Abby called Shawn. She led him to Carly's room. She slid the skinny door open to the secret place. She held her breath.

There was a fluffy puppy wagging its flouncy tail!

Shawn's eyes shone. He sat on the floor and the puppy jumped all over him. He laughed so hard he fell backwards. The puppy stood on his chest and licked his face.

Carly and Jimmy came running. The puppy yipped at them.

"Goody!" said Carly. "Is she ours?"

"We adopted her," said Abby. "But mostly she's Shawn's."

"A good surprise," said Shawn, giggling.

"I can think of two more good surprises." First she looked at Jimmy, then at Shawn. "A double dabble surprise," said Abby.

ABOUT THE AUTHOR

Beverly Lewis remembers waiting for the mail as a kid. She wrote lots of letters to pen pals and other friends. (Still does!)

Beverly and her younger sister, Barbara, had lots of fun with their neighborhood friends. They made "Mushy Goo-Goo"—a secret recipe that included a little water and lots of dirt. They dressed their cats in doll clothes. They hitched up Maxie, their Eskimo Spitz, to a sled and went to the store in a blizzard.

They even had a carnival to raise money for a Jerry's Kids Telethon. And ended up in the newspaper, and later got to be on TV!

If you like books that tickle your funny bone, look for Beverly's next books in the Cul-de-sac Kids series.

Visit Beverly's Web site at *www.BeverlyLewis.com*.

THE CUL-DE-SAC KIDS SERIES

Don't miss #2

CHICKEN POX PANIC

Abby Hunter is planning a birthday cake her brother will never forget. Will she be able to keep it a secret from him? Or will her little sister's big mouth get in the way?

As the party day nears, Abby's best friend, Stacy Henry, needs help solving a mystery. Abby goes broke playing detective. How will she buy the birthday stuff now?

Then, three days before Shawn's party, he breaks out with chicken pox! Abby's in a panic. One by one, the rest of the Cul-de-sac Kids come down with the itchy gitchy pox. What could be worse?

Also by Beverly Lewis

Adult Nonfiction

Amish Prayers
The Beverly Lewis Amish Heritage Cookbook

Adult Fiction

HOME TO HICKORY HOLLOW

The Fiddler • The Bridesmaid • The Guardian
The Secret Keeper • The Last Bride

SEASONS OF GRACE

The Secret • The Missing • The Telling

ABRAM'S DAUGHTERS

The Covenant • The Betrayal • The Sacrifice • The Prodigal
The Revelation

ANNIE'S PEOPLE

The Preacher's Daughter • The Englisher • The Brethren

THE ROSE TRILOGY

The Thorn • The Judgment • The Mercy

THE COURTSHIP OF NELLIE FISHER

The Parting • The Forbidden • The Longing

THE HERITAGE OF LANCASTER COUNTY

The Shunning • The Confession • The Reckoning

OTHER ADULT FICTION

The Postcard • The Crossroad • The Redemption of Sarah Cain
October Song • Sanctuary • The Sunroom • Child of Mine**

Youth Fiction

Girls Only (GO!) Volume One and *Volume Two†*
SummerHill Secrets Volume One and *Volume Two†*
Holly's Heart Collection One‡, Collection Two‡,
and Collection Three†

www.BeverlyLewis.com

*with David Lewis   †4 books in each volume   ‡5 books in each volume

From Bethany House Publishers

Fiction for Young Readers

(ages 7–10)

ASTROKIDS™
by Robert Elmer

Space scooters? Floating robots? Jupiter ice cream? Blast into the future for out-of-this-world, zero-gravity fun with the AstroKids on space station *CLEO-7*.

THE CUL-DE-SAC KIDS
by Beverly Lewis

Each story in this lighthearted series features the hilarious antics and predicaments of nine endearing boys and girls who live on Blossom Hill Lane.

JANETTE OKE'S ANIMAL FRIENDS
by Janette Oke

Endearing creatures from the farm, forest, and zoo discover their place in God's world through various struggles, mishaps, and adventures.